John Stark Colby

Agatha

A Romance of Maine

John Stark Colby

Agatha
A Romance of Maine

ISBN/EAN: 9783337346768

Printed in Europe, USA, Canada, Australia, Japan

Cover: Foto ©Andreas Hilbeck / pixelio.de

More available books at **www.hansebooks.com**

AGATHA

ROMANCE OF MAINE

IN BLANK VERSE

WITH OTHER POEMS

By JOHN STARK COLBY.

"An ill-favored thing, Sir, but mine own."—*As You Like It.*

BOSTON:
A. WILLIAMS & CO.
1880.

To My

MOTHER, WIFE, AND DAUGHTER,

The "Three Graces" of My Life,

THIS VOLUME

IS INSCRIBED.

PREFACE.

"IT was at Lord Murray's table that Sydney Smith told me of
the fun the Edinburgh reviewers used to make of their work. I
taxed him honestly with the mischief they had done by their ferocity
and cruel levity at the outset. It was no small mischief to have
silenced Mrs. Barbauld; and how much more utterance they may
have prevented, there is no saying. It is all very well to talk
sensibly now of the actual importance of reviews, and the real
value of reviewers' judgments; but the fact remains that spirits
were broken, hearts were sickened, and authorship was cruelly
discouraged by the savage and reckless condemnations passed by
the 'Edinburgh Review' in its early days. 'We *were* savage,'
replied Sydney Smith. 'I remember' (and it was plain that he
could not help enjoying the remembrance) 'how Brougham and I
sat trying one night how we could exasperate our cruelty to the
utmost. We had got hold of a poor, nervous little vegetarian,
who had put out a poor, silly little book; and when we had done
our review of it, we sat trying' (and here he joined his finger
and thumb as if dropping from a vial) 'to find one more chink,
one more crevice, through which we might drop in one more drop
of verjuice, to eat into his bones.'" — *Autobiography of Harriet
Martineau.*

CONTENTS.

		PAGE
AGATHA :		
Canto I	. .	9
Canto II	. .	24
Canto III	. .	38
Semi-Centennial of Lowell		55
Illusion	. .	63
Baltimore	. . .	65
Massachusetts and Maryland		71
The Snow	.	79
The Fishers	.	81
Lake Mooselucmaguntic	.	84
To Mount Washington		85
But for a Season	.	86
Drowned	. .	87
Memorial Day	.	89
A Centennial Sentiment	.	94
Fraternity	. . . .	95
Ode to Major-General John Stark		97
Death the Way of Life	. .	101
Time	. . .	104
Christ's Temptation		105
The Golden Rule	.	107
Two Moods	.	109
Mutation	. .	110

" The last of the outrages by the savage tribes .   . broke upon the settle-ments along the Androscoggin above Bethel. In August of 1781 a band of Indians made an attack upon Bethel, and after plundering some of the settlers, and taking others with them as captives, came up through Gilead, murdered one of the hardy settlers there, robbed the cabin of the family that had moved into Shelburne on the snow, and carried their prisoners by Umbagog Lake into Canada." — *The White Hills, by Thos. Starr King.*

AGATHA.

CANTO I.

BRIGHT on the Androscoggin Valley shone
The sun of early autumn. To the south,
From Bethel's teeming intervales, to where
The ceaseless torrent joins the Kennebec, —
Thenceforward mingling till they reach the sea, —
It gleamed upon the husbandman's domain,
The cultivated field, the thrifty town,
And decimated woodlands, fair in death.
To northward, where in deep seclusion lay
The sparkling sources of the mighty stream,
Its rays still fell on virgin wilderness,
Whose native grace had never learned of Art.
Scarce had the universal slayer, Man,
Against defenceless Nature raised his hand,
To prostrate lordly forests on the hills,
Or rob the mountains of their gorgeous hues, —

2

Resplendent with the verdure of the spring,
The green of summer, or more royal tints
Which blaze when lengthened nights have brought the frosts.
Still reared the mountains their Samsonian heads
Unshorn of strength by their Philistine foes.
Not yet through all the solemn, silent aisles
Of God's self-dedicated temples, shrilled
The scream and whistle of the iron steed,
With rumbling train behind, and heavy freight
Of merchandise, — such sacrilege as when
The Jewish doves were bought and sold, till Christ
Drove out the impious brokers, — or of those
Whose souls no homage pay before His shrine.
Primeval peace and beauty reigned supreme.
The brooklets trickled gently down the steeps,
Fed by exhaustless founts which heaven filled,
Fore'er replenishing their wasted store
With miracle as evident from God
As that His prophet wrought, in ancient time,
Upon the widow's meal and cruse of oil.
The breezes softly stirred among the trees,
That quivered with respondent ecstasy,
E'en as the mother's heart beats joyously
When on her lips her first-born prints a kiss.
All that was less than perfect was such mark
As ever doth pertain to finite works :
Like tears, and sighs, and weakness of the babe,
Scarce less than angel, ere foul sin by stealth
Admittance gains and innocence is slain.

Beside a lucid brook, which all the day
Sang blithesomely, as swiftly on it sped,
A single settler reared his humble cot,
Of rough-hewn timber: one whose love intense
Of quietude, had led him in advance
Of frontier yeomen, to seek here a home
Removed from turmoil of the border-town;
Whom, neither, city life did please, with cares
And competitions for his needful bread.
So here he found a refuge, well content
With seeing no face but his faithful wife's
And happy children's; only love dwelt there,
But elsewhere cold and distant look, mistrust,
Or worse; for all his other kin were dead.
Here had his sturdy arm dealt fatal blows,
With keen-edged axe, to many a mighty oak,
And lofty pine, and cedar, for a space
To plant his crops; and under smiling skies,
He prospered well, and thanked his God for all.
Few were his wants and those of all his house;
Their fare, the product of their fruitful land,
With fish from out the rill, game from the wood,
And seasonings of least luxurious sort,
Obtained from Indian bands, or huntsmen stray,
Who at rare intervals that way would pass:
And twice or thrice a year he pilgrimaged
For leagues amid the pathless wilds around,
The sun his guide, for requisite supplies,
Secured by barter at some settlement.

Thus happily had passed the swift-shod months,
With no disturbance of their tranquil lot,
No shattered hopes, no racking jealousies,
No burning fever of ambitious schemes,
No blasting sickness, want, nor visit dire
Of the remorseless archer, fearful Death.
They envied not the mighty, for they reigned
Unchallenged in the affections of their loved ;
Nor coveted the riches of the proud,
For they were blest with plenty ; nor would wish
For Eden's Garden to enhance their joys.

Alas ! how fate bemocks our wisest plans,
And when we fain some evil would evade,
From our endeavor works that very ill !
So he, who fled from haunt of men, to gain
Assured relief from strife, and certain end
Of diabolic passions, fell a prey
To savages, whose breasts no pity knew.

The autumn sun descended with a glow ;
The twilight gently gathered in the sky ;
The birdlings ceased their piping on the boughs ;
The tired children turned them from their sports,
To warm themselves beside the kitchen fire ;
The mother spread the modest evening meal,
Her infant soothing with a lullaby ;
The weary father laid aside his tools,
And homeward plodded from his daily task ;

The darkness deepened ; and the twinkling stars
Looked down upon a scene of sweet repose.
From off its resting-place, the Bible plain,
With well-worn lids and pages soiled with use,
The settler took ; and there he read of Him
Who life immortal to the world revealed.
Then bowed they down to pray, and rose, and sought
Their welcome couches, dreaming of no harm.

What cry was that which hurtled through the night
Upon their startled slumbers?   Did the wolves
Within the distant thickets, fasting long,
Their ravening hunger seek to satisfy?
Or was the angry she-bear now abroad,
In quest of victims for her yelping brood ?
Perchance the wanton catamount doth roam
Within the valley — monster dreaded most
By red-skinned hunter and pale-face alike.
Ah, no !   A more insatiate foe than these,
More potent and relentless, stood without.
Scarce had the frightened woodsman time to sob —
" The Indians are upon us ! — wife, arise !
Flee out into the darkness with the babe !
Mayhap you shall escape them, while with Ralph
And Eva I another course will try " —
When with a horrid din the door was burst ;
The painted, shouting, blood-encurdling crew,
Not ghastlier had they fresh from hell's dark caves
Ascended, to the chamber forced their way.

And, as the fainting mother clasped her child
Convulsive in her terror, they with force
Disparted from her arms their precious weight ;
Then as she struggled, hopeless, yet with strength
New-born of frenzy, far beyond her sex,
The brutal deed was tragically closed
By plunging 'mid her dark, disheveled locks
The gleaming, fatal tomahawk of steel.
Nor fared the husband safer : in his breast,
As weaponless he fought, a knife was sheathed,
And lifeless lay he, reeking in his gore.
The children, speechless, view the awful crime
With varying emotions. Ralph, the lad,
O'er whom the seasons of ten years have passed,
Beholds the gaping wounds and crimson streams
With tears of woe and fear. The eldest girl,
Scarce four years old, from face to face appeals,
But sees in all incarnate demonism,
And, loudly weeping, casts herself beside
The body of her mother, cold in death ;
There, blotting out the frightful spectacle,
She hides her face within the ample folds
Of garments blood-besmeared, and moans her grief.
The tender infant, rudely borne about,
Croons with amazement, or with terror cries,
Alternate smiles and shrieks upon her lips.
These three are spared, and forth into the night
Are hurried ; while about the squatter's cot
Bright-blazing faggots are anon applied.

The mounting flames envelop it about
With quick destruction; and as Ralph one glance
Throws back upon his childhood's joyous home,
It crumbles into embers. Then his steps
Are harshly quickened by his captors fierce.
So haste they forward through the gloomy depths,
No word exchanged, save when some low command
In unknown accent is announced, till gray
The eastern sky grows with the coming dawn.
The dry leaves rustle sadly under-foot;
The wind soughs mournfully among the pines;
No other sound but notes of waking birds,
The light footfalls upon the frosty earth,
And snapping twigs, along the course they trend.
With daylight, now the boy discerns the throng
Consists of many dusky-visaged braves,
In all their native hideous array.
No women of their own dark race appeared;
But, scattered here and there, poor Ralph beheld
Of captives like himself, in wild despair,
A motley troop: frail women, half-enrobed,
With pinioned hands behind them, feet thorn-pierced,
Limbs bruised and bleeding, clothing torn and rent, —
Whose choking sobs not e'en their enemies
Could stifle, nor their feeble, flagging pace
With blows and threats enough accelerate;
And children of all ages, sexes both,
Made sudden orphans in a single hour,
And doomed to end their days in savagery.

But now his sinking heart awhile revived
At seeing in the arms of one he knew,
His youngest infant sister, sound and hale,
Though full of worriment and baby-grief.
Borne by a stalwart half-breed youth was she,
Whom Ralph had met at times in former days,
Beside his father's hearth, in milder guise.
To her he ventured his accustomed voice,
To calm her wailing ; when upon his cheek
Smote sharply one who led him ; and he ceased.

At length the fleeing band came to a halt
Within a vale secluded, where a brook
Poured forth its plaintive gurgle on the air.
Exhausted by their long and rapid march,
The foot-sore captives prone upon the ground
Sank, well-nigh helpless ; while the Indian host
Prepared a hurried meal of yellow maize
And meat of wild-deer, in the sun's rays dried.
No fire they built, lest by its curling smoke
Some chance intruder, or pursuing white,
Should learn where they encamped, and vengeance bring.
Short was the pause.   The meagre breakfast o'er,
A council gathered by itself apart.
Their words to Ralph were barren, but their tone,
Their bodeful gestures, and their furtive glance
Betokened to the captives dismal hap,
Too soon revealed ; for, spite of tears and prayers,
The weaker women and the helpless babes

Were, in the very presence of their friends,
Despatched with heartless fury. Ralph turned sick
And swooned, to see the dread atrocity, —
To see the half-breed, who his sister held,
Him who had shared his father's bounty oft,
Into the water toss the moaning child,
That but a moment floated, then was whelmed.

Again to consciousness the boy awoke,
Called by a summons to resume the flight.
He saw the fugitives in twain divide :
One party to the northward turned their steps,
While he and those about him journeyed west.
Each company a share of captives took,
Distributed by lot. Ralph vainly hoped
To recognize his sister Eva once.
Not since the nightmare scene within their home,
When pallid in the moonlight on the floor
He saw her, screening in their mother's dress
Her piteous eyes, had he beheld her face.
And now he doubted not her death, but thought
That him alone, of all the household dear,
These barbarous executioners had spared.
He wept in secret, for he shrank from death,
Nor dared display retributive intent ;
But in his inmost soul he vowed an oath,
If e'er occasion came, to have revenge
On him who, in his aching sight, had slain,
With ruthless hand, his sister Juliet.

3

Yet little consolation drew he thence ;
For Half-Breed Jack (by that uncertain name
Alone he knew the ruffian) had withdrawn
With those who disappeared, he knew not where,
Within the shady coverts of the wood
To northward.   So he nursed his grief and hate,
Compliant outwardly to every beck
And signal of his captors.   Thus the day
In tedious tramping slowly turned to night.

The spot selected for the evening camp —
A glade upon a grassy, wood-girt hill —
Gave promise of an undisturbed repose.
On one side flowed a rill, with murmur soft ;
Above, the firmament was full in view,
With all its myriads of shining orbs ;
Exposed all day to vivifying heat,
The turfy carpet had not yet grown brown,
But summer's grateful freshness lingered still.
Beside the streamlet's brink a fire was built.
Where straightway was the rude repast prepared.
The brands were then extinguished in the brook ;
For, though long distance had been traversed o'er,
Without a sign to indicate pursuit,
The wary band preserved a cautious care.
They posted sentries vigilant, to guard
The captives and prevent surprise ; then sleep
The senses of the many quick possessed.
There, as they lay beneath the cold, blue sky,

Which seemed to hold no pity for his lot,
Ralph pondered long upon his altered state,
And wondered if the spirits of the dead —
Of those whom he had lost so soon before —
Knew aught of his condition, or could help.
Then said that prayer, which, by his mother taught,
He had so often whispered at her knee.
So came to mind the sayings of that Book
He loved ; and to the promise now he clung :
" Unto the fatherless a Father I
Will be " ; and, hope reviving, so he slept.

Slept, to awaken 'mid a tumult wild,
Confusion of swift-rushing feet, loud cries,
And musket-shots, and clash of warlike arms ;
Arose affrighted, to behold a strife
Of struggling foe with foe, in deadly grasp,
Or fleeing helter-skelter to the wood ;
While all about the glade could he detect
Dark, shapeless masses, where the fallen lay.
The horrid scene he comprehended not.
Perchance he dreamt ; perchance some hostile tribe
Of stealthy warriors, wandering this way,
Had lighted on the camp, with hope to kill
The whole unconscious, unsuspecting group.
So, solving not his fear-producing doubts,
He, trembling, fell again upon the earth,
And closed his troubled eyes, and clasped his hands,
And tried to banish all the hateful sight.

In vain ! He cowered there in agony,
Expecting death, which coyly held aloof,
As if, like some blood-thirsty beast of prey,
It fain would tease its victim for a spell,
And tantalizing hope impart, at last
To crush him with one herculean stroke.
He craved it so might prove ; for he had drained,
He felt, affliction's cup till naught was left.
But heaven ordained a longer lease of days,
And further miseries, yet not unmixed
With gracious blessings, such as men most prize.
For, after he had lain in silence long, —
How long he could not reckon, if he would, —
His spirit heard, as in a kind of trance,
The accents of his own familiar speech.
Nor from a fellow-bondsman did they come :
It was the language of authority,
Though kindly uttered, that his glad ear caught.
He felt himself removed from off the earth,
And oped his eyes, to gaze upon a friend, —
For, sure, that countenance no malice held,
Though strange to him, and stern, and deeply bronzed.
Deliverance, he knew, had come at last,
And all his pent-up feelings found a voice.

     The fact was soon disclosed.   A hardy corps
Of yeomen volunteers, from near and far, —
To whom intelligence of Indian raid
Against the settlers had been slowly brought

By one who 'scaped the wholesale massacre, —
Had followed on the trail, espied the camp,
Concealed their presence with consummate skill
Until an hour propitious for the charge,
And thus had wrested from the clan their prey.
Nor ceased they there: but with the sword and fire
Had slaughtered many, — scattered all beside, —
And dealt retaliation for their crimes.
Yet with a desperation worthy fiends,
Who revel in the anguish of the lost,
The savages, when of defeat aware,
Had butchered all their captives saving Ralph.
Him back to liberty his saviors bore;
And, pitying his lorn and orphaned case
(For that an only son not long before
They had themselves consigned to native dust),
The leader and his gentle wife resolved
To rear him and adopt him as their own.
His years were tender ; and, though on his mind
The harsh experience of his early life
Had wrought impressions ne'er to be effaced,
He soon forgot his melancholy state,
Returned his benefactors love for love,
And grew in their regard, in youthful grace,
In public confidence and moral worth.
Amid Pequaket's [1] hills and glades and farms, —
The former home of Paugus and his tribe,

---

[1] The aboriginal name of Fryeburg, Me., and vicinity.

Till Chamberlain sent home the whizzing ball, —
He passed his time with profit at his books,
Learned wisdom in the schools, yet not alone
From sources such as these he gathered lore :
For many times communed he face to face
(Though not with eyes of flesh he could discern,
As Moses on the smoking mount) with God
Upon the crest of princely Kiarsarge. —
Fit as Olympus, or as Sinai's self,
For Him whose canopy is cloud and fire ;
Oft heard, as guilty Adam shrank to hear,
The Lord of Nature, in the cool of day,
Amid the groves in zephyrs whisper low ;
Oft caught an inspiration fresh from heav'n
From that fair lake which imaged the blue vault ;
Of day learned speech, from night rare knowledge drew,
As sky and earth united to declare
The glories of their Maker and Support ;
And throve so well, that in his eighteenth year
His martial patron gained for him access
To West Point, where to learn of rugged war.
There sped the months on velvet feet away,
As ever in bright youth their custom is,
Till graduation led Ralph far away —
A handsome, brave lieutenant — to the West,
To battle for his country and for fame.
In Indian campaign saw he bloody deeds ;
In exploration passed securer weeks ;
In scientific expedition joined,

And into Nature's grandest secrets peered.
He stood upon the everlasting peaks,
Where storms had raged for ages all untold :
He threaded wilderness till then untrod ;
His soul drank tull of Nature's majesty,
Expanding day by day within her realm ;
He viewed her wonders, worshipped at her feet,
Yet recognized beyond a Hand Divine.

CANTO II.

Far in the wilds of Canada remote,
Within a fertile valley, broad and fair,
Thick-wooded, watered, and from fervid sun
And wintry blast protected in degree,
A wigwam village nestled 'mid the trees.
A troop of sinewy youths, engaged in sports,
Made merry clamor on the tranquil air,
As one performed some feat of skill, or strove
Successfully a rival to surpass.
Here wrestled twain, with dextrous play of strength ;
There other two ran swiftly o'er the lea,
For triumph striving as for very life,
Though all the meed of victory should be
A murmur of approval from grave men,
A cheery nod from beldams, or (rare prize!)
A smile and look of pride from some shy lass.
Those shot the arrow at a distant mark,
While others leaped, or lifted cumbrous weights ;—
Each athlete zealous to secure applause.
Apart from these, sedate and self-reserved,
A group of warriors sat beneath the shade,

Engrossed in council, while the atmosphere
Grew fragrant with the incense of their pipes.
Here rollicked on the earth, in scanty garb
Or destitute of raiment, children swarth,
Whose laughter, floating on the soft south wind,
With other sounds commingled and expired.
A few sleek dogs stole silently about,
Or dozed without concern ;—all signs of life
Betrayed contentment and a quiet lot.

But, stay ! Secluded in the leafy grove,
At distance from the village and its scenes,
Behold two strange companions, lone and sad.
Why do they differ in their mood and guise
From all who dwell in the adjacent town ?
Why are their cheeks without the copper stain,
Their tresses silken and of texture fine ?
For many leagues no settlement exists
Besides the Indian hamlet; whence, then, come
This pale-browed woman and this timid girl ?
List ! for the elder speaks in tone subdued,
As to her mate she breathes the oft-heard tale :
"Sweet maiden, by thy rightful name thou art
To me unknown, though daughter thou hast been
To one of offspring prematurely reft.
Two darling children and a husband fond
Long years ago I happily could claim ;
But all, our Heavenly Father, — nay, not so !
Say, rather, Satan dwelling in the flesh,

4

As once God suffered him to visit Job, —
In few brief hours transferred from my embrace ;
And as I prayed that I might follow them,
But in His wisdom God denied the boon,
Mine eyes were turned on thee ; and soon there sprang
Within my breast a love for thee intense.
The Fates were gracious ; thou unto my charge
Wast given by our captors ; and thy name,
From them derived, was called 'The Nightingale.'
Thy lineage and birthplace, if they know,
Our masters reticent have ne'er divulged.
With us were driven to this hated place
Still other prisoners in wretched plight,
Whom thou may'st call to mind ; but thou and I
Alone now live, of all that dismal train ;
O'ercome by miseries so manifold,
They one by one have welcomed death's relief.
Ten weary years my bruised heart has sustained,
And I would linger still for thy dear sake,
But now I feel that I shall soon be called
To join my loved ones in the Summer Land ;
Then thou wilt here remain without one friend.
Ah, bitter and despiteful lot !   The days
Will slowly o'er thy burdened spirit pass,
Till thou art summoned to the Angel World.
O precious soul ! if thou mightst go with me
On that mysterious journey I must take,
How gladly would I yield my fleeting breath ! "
Her choking sobs no further would permit

Her discourse ; clasped in one another's arms,
The speaker and the listener wept aloud.
Then, when a spell their tears had mingled thus,
The younger said : " No mother but thyself
Can I recall, from childhood till this hour.
Indeed, a benefaction hast thou been,
Without whom life were joyless as the grave.
My kindred's speech in secret thou has taught,
Their solacing religion, and their God.
To part from thee forever, — here to stay,
The solitary vestige of my race, —
Were bitterer than all the pangs of death,
And only less than hell in final hope.
Say, must thou die ?   And, if so, may I not
Existence by mine own will terminate ? "
Again they wept ; but soon the other spoke :
"Our Savior, when on earth, declared that He,
And only He, had power over life.
He suffered ignominy worse than thine,
And poignant tortures preyed upon his soul ;
Yet fled He not the ordeal, but endured,
Till blessed dissolution set Him free.
'No murder shalt thou do,' is sternly writ,
And 'He that murders hath not endless life.'
Then seek not so thy hardships to avert,
Lest haply unknown evils lurk beyond.
'God doth not willingly afflict nor grieve ';
Some purpose hath He when He trieth us ;
Forbear thy hand, and 'do thyself no harm ' !

But not of succor need'st thou quite despair.
A child thou art; some chance may ope the door
To free thee, ere the gloomy tomb thou reach.
The Red Men naught suspect thee; thou dost go
Untrammeled wheresoe'er thy wishes prompt.
In future years there may occur to thee
Auspicious opportunity for flight
Beyond their vengeance, or thy countrymen
May save thee from them; but essay thou not
To penetrate alone the dreary wilds,
Unbroken by the people of thy blood
For countless leagues; for thou wouldst perish there
Of hunger, or by beasts, or deadly cold,
Or peradventure fall a victim dire
To those who would pursue thee and o'ertake.
Have patience, pray thee, till kind Providence,
In pity for thy weakness and distress,
Shall send an earthly or a heavenly guide!"

But here their colloquy abruptly closed.
They heard approaching footsteps, and in haste
They sought to hide all traces of their grief;
Their tears they staunched; the words of their lament
Ceased straightway o'er their quivering lips to flow;
They rose from their recumbent attitude
And turned their faces villageward to go.
Their purpose thus divining, gruffly cried
The interloper, as he darkly frowned:

' "Why do you shun my presence? I am one
Who ever strive to please you and befriend ;
I fain would do you kindness; but ye shrink,
When I draw near, as doth the trembling fawn
Before the greedy wolf or skulking bear.
I would not harm you, for in truth I love
The Nightingale, and for her sake her mate."
The maiden's cheek blanched white as driven snow,
While insolently smote her ears these words;
Her palpitating bosom needed not
Interpretation by her speechless tongue ;
With indignation and with loathing fear
Her form was shaken like the aspen-leaf.
Th' intruder paused, then, by an impulse moved,
Advanced to where the girl in silence stood,
And from her lips he sought to steal a kiss.
Though seen but late, the effort she eludes,
And steps aside, abhorrent at his act ;
Then slips away and leaves him wholly foiled.
"Aha !" he gasps, in voice of stifled wrath,
"I yet shall win you, though I woo you not.
'T was I that saved you from untimely end
And brought you hither when a tender child.
Within my veins there courses blood like yours,
And you should look with favor on my suit.
But if you still resist, 't is all in vain ;
By right of might I yet will grace my tent
With you as mistress, subject to my will !"

Then, deigning neither word nor look to her
(The woman), who scarce yet had dared to stir,
He turned upon his heel and disappeared.

When now her friend the breathless girl regained,
The menace was repeated as o'erheard ;
At which, with tears renewed, the frightened maid
Sobbed, " Save me, mother, from that ruffian's clutch,
Or I to desperate means shall make resort !"
With thoughts of comfort her the elder cheered,
And so they reached their primitive abode.

The tedious winter, with its sifting storms,
Its freezing and its loud-complaining winds,
Its barren forests, save the sombre green
Which hardy fir and pine and hemlock wear,
Hath now seized all the land in its embrace.
The lakes and rivers are congealed to ice ;
The earth is thickly mantled with the snows,
And far below its surface lurk the frosts ;
All Nature's forces seem well-nigh expired,
Or in confinement held and bolted fast.
The dwellers in the hamlet feed their fires
With massive back-logs and with faggots dry,
Impatiently awaiting genial spring.
By day they spend their leisure in the hunt ;
Or through the ice they spear their finny prey ;
Or deftly weave lithe thongs on seasoned frames,
Whereby they glide above the yielding drifts,

Which clog the floundering moose and prove its doom ;
Or skilfully their bark canoes construct,
To float serenely on broad lake and stream
When once again the sun shall loose their thrall.
By night, beside their ruddy, gleaming hearths,
They chant wild songs of bloodshed and of love,
Tell wondrous stories, or in games of chance
With revel coarse they pass the tardy hours.

The shades of evening now are darkly drawn ;
A howling tempest through the valley sweeps,
As in one tent a mournful group surround
The pallet where a dying mortal lies.
The flickering embers cast a sickly gloom
Athwart the features of the sufferer,
And by the partial light we may descry
That this is she of Nightingale beloved.
And there beside her kneels the sobbing girl,
One hand caressing 'mid convulsive grief.
More faintly comes and goes the vital breath :
More fixed and stony grow the sunken eyes ;
More feeble are the pulse-beats, till at last,
With one deep sigh, the spirit flits away
From out its clayey prison into bliss.
Poor child ! thine earthly consolation fails ;
In this world none canst thou now claim to be
A mother or a friend, to guard from ill ;
The sepulchre shall swallow all thy hope,
And in a living tomb thy heart shall throb !

Again the vivifying smile of spring
Awakes the buds and lures the songsters back
To haunts forsaken erst for warmer clime.
Th' unfettered brooks perpetual praises raise,
That they are free to gambol as they will ;
The morning matin and the vesper hymn
Ascend to the Creator from His works ;
And only man, His proudest offspring, dares
Withhold meet tribute and obedience due.

Rejoicing that their pent-up, dull camp-life
Shall be supplanted by more active modes,
Fresh animation beams on every face.
And cheerful sounds re-echo through the glen.
But chiefly jubilant of all the braves
Is he who yonder rears his wigwam new,
Adorned with trophies which his valiant hands
Have won from savage foe, in war or chase.
The sloping walls consist of wild-beasts' hide ;
The earth is softly carpeted with pelts
From furry victims of the trapper's art ;
While all about, barbaric ornaments
Bedeck the canopy or strew the floor.
Nor doth the owner's prowess sole appear
From spoils of beasts that cause stout hearts to quail :
Long tresses, dangling full in sight, declare
The gory conquests which his arm has gained.
But hourly, as the lodge completion nears,
And ever, as her eye beholds the work,

One heart stops beating, one brain madly whirls,
One face turns ashen as the livid dead.
The bride-elect, — the lovely Nightingale, —
For whom the half-white warrior blithely builds,
Forebodes her coming fate with nameless dole.
The last day dawns ; the last touch is applied ;
The domicile awaits its mistress fair,
Whom he that formed it shall to-morrow claim
To be his spouse, with merry bout and feast.
O Thou who reignest in the distant skies,
Against such consummation interpose!

When deep the world is plunged in gloom of night,
A figure pauses by the river's brink,
A slender shape, with agitation swept.
As noiselessly as Charon on the Styx
His barge propels, when with a muffled stroke
He ferries chattering ghosts to Hades' shore,
She launches on the stream her bark canoe.
The paddle grasps, and swiftly disappears.
The sacrilege designed shall never be ;
The Right shall triumph, spite of every odds.
For prayers are heard of Him who rules the world ;
Iniquity, though seated on a throne,
Supported by a kingdom's might and wealth,
Is impotent against His fiat just.
Then fear not, feeble maiden !   Have thou faith !
In thine own strength is failure ; but on high
A Guardian and Protector thou shalt have.

5

Speed thou with courage o'er the trackless waste !
As oft the pinions of the timid bird
By unseen Hand are piloted aright
From bleak north country to the balmy south,
So thou, far higher than the sparrow loved,
Shalt safely be conducted unto rest !

The early morn brought news to all the tribe
That Nightingale had fled.   The surly groom,
With disappointment chafing, hid his ire,
Beseeching none to follow but himself ;
Alone, he boasted, he would bring her home
Within three days, and then the nuptial rites
Should be the gayer for the brief delay.
He said, and ready acquiescence met ;
Then cast his practised eye from point to point,
Soon traced her footsteps to the river-sands,
And saw the keel-marks of the missing boat.
Of others like it there were many near ;
He quickly thrust one in the current swift,
Its light oars wielding with a giant force ;
The fragile craft skimmed lightly o'er the wave,
Till past the reach of vision it had sped.

With straining muscles, all the star-lit night,
Frail Nightingale had madly rowed her skiff ;
But when the rosy sunrise found her weak,
Her strength o'ertaxed, her blistered hands becramped,
Her body, from its unaccustomed toil

And lack of food and sleep, exhausted quite,
Then first seemed vain and rash her bold attempt.
Before, she had not reasoned; crazed with dread,
She sought relief instinctively in flight;
But now she realized the solemn fact
That foes would seek, would find her, and return
To more intolerable slavery
Than she before had known; for, from henceforth,
Suspicion would attend her future state.
She ceased her efforts and to grief gave vent,
While gently onward drifted her canoe,
As though it fain would distance all pursuit.
Thus passed the long forenoon; on berries ripe
Which grew upon the bank she broke her fast,
And so in part her famishment appeased.
At times, as yet no follower appeared,
Her sinking hope revived; she then would urge
Her course, though ever with diminished power;
And often backward threw distrustful glance,
Expectant of the climax and the end.

The sun was trending slowly tow'rd the west,
The heat of mid-day had declined apace,
And o'er her wearied senses 'gan to steal
The soft encroachments of unbidden sleep,
When of a sudden on her startled ear
Crept sounds that chilled and paralyzed her heart.
No longer subtle slumber weaves its spell;
Her temples throb well-nigh to bursting; low

She bends her head and lists with bated breath.
Ah, me! 'tis true! Her most distressing doubt
Meets sad fulfilment in that fatal hour;
The rapid plashing of an oarsman's strokes
Distinctly breaks the stillness of the wood.
One moment later, and her blood-shot eyes
Behold the cause of her tormenting fears;
With wild halloo he makes the forest ring,
As with redoubled energy he rows.
No more her unnerved frame can bear; her hands
Fall listless at her side; the slender oar
Slips from her clasp and quickly floats away;
Her eyelids droop and close; across her lips
A shrill cry issues, and she fainting falls,
Her face all colorless as marble white;
Her weight o'erturns the frail canoe; she sinks
Beneath the gurgling waters, and is lost.

But, no! Though thus she might have wished to die,
And peacefully awake where nevermore
Adversity and sorrow might obtrude,
But only joy supernal have a place;
Not so her destiny decreed, — not so
Would he permit who followed in her wake.
In one brief moment he had reached the spot
Where she had been engulfed; and, with a bound,
He plunged beneath the surface, in his arms
Enfolded her within a strong embrace,
And brought her form inanimate to shore.

"My pledge I yet will keep," he muttered then ;
"My pretty bird, not three days shall elapse
Since you betrayed our trust and flew away,
Before I have you in mine own nest safe!"
He gently chafed her unresisting palms,
Her wrists he stroked, and kissed her moistened brow.
She groaned, as wretched life returned to her,
But knew not yet if this were life or death,
Till on her shuddering gaze his image stood,
Whereat a second time she swooned.
                                        But what
Hath caused the half-breed on his feet to leap,
As with electric shock?   A horrid oath
Escaped him, and a hurried look he cast
Behind him, whence proceeded near at hand
The detonations of a horse's hoofs.
He had no time for flight; so deep-absorbed
In efforts he had been to wake the lass,
He failed to note the sound until too late.
A clarion voice commanded, and forthwith
His arms were pinioned by a dozen men,
Whose uniform he knew full well, and cursed.
They led him straightway to their rude abode ;
There safely bound him ; and he saw them bear
The half-unconscious maiden to a tent.

CANTO III.

As sweeps the flame across some prairie sere,
Ignited from a careless herder's camp;
The smoke in murky clouds mounts to the sky,
And thousand wild-beasts flee in blindest haste;
Their cries and thund'rous trampling sound afar:
So swiftly through the village sped the tale
Of Nightingale's release, and how her foe,
The dark-skinned alien, had been captive brought.
Not more sensation had there been, for sure,
Had proclamation been announced of peace
Between the young Republic and the Crown:
For these had drawn the sword, and war's rude blows
Had dealt each other, now these many months,
By land and ocean; which, incarnadined,
Appealed to heaven for that promised day
When Man no more shall wield the deadly sword.
For this cause, forth from out the pleasant town
Had marched a sturdy squad of chosen souls,
Ralph being in command, through Northern wilds,
Crossed Canada's frontier, on havoc bent,

And so had come at juncture opportune
To save the maiden from her enemy.
Him to the jail they bore; while she found rest
Within the selfsame home where Ralph, a child,
Had been received as son, and fondly reared.
There tarried she for many days, till passed
The anguish of her trials, and her heart,
Warmed with the kindness of her new-found friends,
Leaped out in artless gratitude and trust.
They, too, beheld this object of their grace
With deep compassion; and the matron said:
"No daughter hath the Lord possessed me with;
So this poor waif shall live with me, and cheer
My lonely hours with dear companionship.
And let her AGATHA be called; 't is meet
That one so pure and good should bear that name."
So one and all assented, not least pleased
The youthful hero, though the reason why
He scarce suspected; for he knew no throb
Of tender passion, but of glory dreamed.

Then, after long contention, tidings came
Of amity between the nations twain.
No more should widows mourn, and orphans weep,
And parents shed the tear, for loved ones laid
In distant grave unmarked, or plunged adown
The yawning depths of the insatiate sea.
The hideous furies hied themselves away

To nether world, sole dwelling-place befit
For such as take delight in deeds of blood.
Emancipation sought the half-breed out;
But he, professing penitence and wish
To recompense the wrong he had essayed,
Remained and earned precarious livelihood
In labor for the farmers, or he wrought
Quaint trinkets with barbaric skilfulness.

  Meanwhile the girl doth prosper in her ways;
Her books were pastime; and with voice so rich
Had nature dowered her, that all who heard
Were raptured by its siren quality,
E'en though the melody were strange, and words
Uncouth, as when she sang some Indian chant;
Or, profited by cultivation, when
She thrilled the village church with sacred praise.
Her beauteous face reflected guileless heart;
Her eyes of azure beamed with innocence;
Her rounded figure, ruddy, dimpled cheeks,
And deep-brown ringlets, ranked her leading belle,
At whose approach the pulse of many a youth
Beat quick and hectic, with emotion deep.

  Once more brusque winter broods the earth above;
The joyous holidays draw on apace
When all discomforts of the outer world
Are reckoned naught; when severed families
Unite again around one common hearth,

And merry laughter tells of happy homes,
Whence care is banished for a little while.
Then Ralph is welcomed to a short reprieve
From dangers of his frontier life; and oft
He stirs their hearts with tales of sharp dismay.
Thus while he speaks, the eyes of Agatha
Are fixed upon the floor, while half-breathed sighs,
Not unperceived, escape her coral lips.
With furtive glance Ralph strives to read the truth;
For, since they parted last, her absent shape
Has flitted, day and night, before the view
Of his abstracted mind, — her hath he found
More precious to his soul than all beside
Of high ambition or exalted hope.
Not so unkind were Fate, to blast his fame,
As to deprive him of her saintly face;
Not more distraught, if 'on a sea-girt isle
Alone he wandered, could he feel himself,
If Agatha divided not his lot.

And so, one eve, into her willing ear
He told the story, pleading for return
Of his attachment, as a culprit might
For sweet existence on the scaffold's brink ;
The while wise-blinking stars, as ages long
They have been privileged, looked down and heard
The plighted troth of one more mated pair, —
To whom that hour was revelation rare
And new and perfect, as when Adam's bride

6

Came to him first from God's creative hand.
What deep felicity the ransomed know,
Assuredly no human eye hath seen ;
But nothing of our mortal state more near
Approacheth to the heavenly than the joy
Of lovers, when they pledge their early faith :
These, with ecstatic vision, e'er behold
The world invested with a halo new.

Their mutual choice revealed, with plaudit met ;
E'en those who envied, recognized how fit
The two were for each other, and resigned
To manifest decree of higher powers.
Yet, while rejoicing reigned, there came a pang
Of sadness unto Agatha and Ralph ;
For he was bound by honor and by law
To serve his country further under arms ;
And though she proffered — ay, demanded it —
To join him in his rough campaigning, he
Forbade the sacrifice, and showed its ills,
Till she desisted. Then it was resolved
That for one year — a trifling space of time,
Yet, ah ! how much within a year befalls —
He should alone hie to the Western plains,
While she should cross the sea to foreign lands
And blithely sing the slow-paced weeks away ;
But ere they thus should part, they would be wed.
Then, lapsed the interval, they both should turn

Their faces homeward, and be henceforth all
To one another, till the hour of death.

   The merry sands of the expiring year
Sped swiftly to oblivion; came the dawn
Of its successor, and thus all too soon
The dismal day when they must say " Farewell!"
The two stood side by side, environed round
By friends, within the parlor of the ship
That presently should waft the bride afar.
The sacred service of the Church was said,
And blessing on them breathed, as man and wife,
By reverend lips; and then, 'mid smiles and tears
And gratulations from the gladsome throng,
One lingering embrace they took, — one kiss
Ralph fixed upon her chill, pain-stricken cheek, —
One lisp of comfort and of future hope
Bespoke; next resolutely turned to shore,
Assuming cheerful mien and word not felt.
Convulsive sobs, the bride could ill repress,
But for her husband's sake concealed, the while.
And so they separated.   Down the bay
The noble vessel drifted, till strained eyes
No longer could discern on deck or wharf
The clouded countenance or signal hand.
Then all the bitterness of sundered hearts
The pair experienced; but new courage rose,
As peered their vision forward, and they saw
A glorious bow of promise span their sky.

But what dark-scowling face is this that Ralph
Beholds beside him as he turns to go,
His fair young wife no longer visible?
What pent-up malice in that leering eye
Is now to burst upon him?   Mute, there stands
The Indian; and Ralph cries, in sudden dread,
"Whence have you come?   Why are you here to-day?
Speak, and reveal your rankling, inmost thoughts!"
The other, slowly, and with sarcasm, raised
The single query, "Married?" — while a shrug
Of evil portent seemed more loud to speak
The secret mischief of his wicked heart.
"Yes; praised be God!   This day I wedded her
Whom thou, foul wretch, didst once dare hope to hold
In thy base clutch.   Avaunt from out my sight,
Or chastisement severe my hand shall deal!
Thine evil presence strangely angers me."
Thus hotly spake the bridegroom, while a flash
Malignant shot from underneath the brow
Of the despised and sullen outcast.   Then
He ground his teeth, and made reply in words
That burned into the hearer's very brain:
"Think not, proud white man, you shall always win!
The hawk that pounces on the basking snake,
Aloft may bear it in his talons' grasp,
Till, writhing in its pain, the prey may strike
Its soaring captor with a mortal sting."
"Dost thou threat me, vile craven of thy race, —
Or, rather, one without a race on earth,

With blood compounded of the meanest dregs?
If self-respect would warrant such descent
To thine own level, by the gods above!
This moment would I let the current out,
And drench the ground to nausea with its filth.
Get thee from out my sight, and proffer thanks
That thou escapest with thy caitiff life!"
"Hear me one moment, yet!" the Indian hissed:
"Dost thou remember of thy childhood's home?—
The purling brook, beside which all the day
Thou playedst with thy sister, or alone
Pursu'dst with rod and line for speckled trout?
Canst thou recall the clearing, and the cot,
Surrounded by the tall and piney wood?
Of father and of mother doth thy mind
Still hold remembrance, and their image see,
Ere Red Men from the Northland stole their life?
Didst thou not have an infant sister, too?
Were not she and the elder shrieking borne
With thee into the darkness of that night,
When fell thy father's cabin by the brand?
Ay! well canst thou bring back to mind these scenes,
Though years have lapsed since all were swept away.
Know, then, that I remember this, as well;
I saw thee often near that selfsame hut,
And sometimes shared thy childish gambollings.
I stood where I beheld the flames devour
The cottage and its owner.   I am he
Whom thou, in boyhood, hail'dst as Half-Breed Jack!"

"Good God! thou liest!   O, confess me now,
That thou hast harrowed up my soul in jest,
And I can cheerfully forgive!" gasped Ralph.
"Here — take this money!   Tell me this is false
That thou hast uttered, and in me a friend
In after years thou evermore shalt find."
"Put up thy gift; I scorn it as I do
The giver!" cried the savage.   "I have watched
And waited long for vengeance on thy head.
Now — now I have it, and I find it sweet
As store of wild-bees to the starving bear.
One revelation more thine ear shall catch;
And if it slay thee, or thou goest mad,
I will gloat o'er thee as the thirsting wolf
Above its hapless victim of the fold:
Thy sister Eva thou hast wed to-day!
Ha, ha!   Thy sister thou dost call thy wife!"
"Thou worse than liar! worse than murderer!
Thus to invent these hellish tales, and mock
My dearest hopes and sole felicity!
Fiend, who transcendest in thy matchless hate
That cursed people — cursed of God and man —
Whom Heaven's Great Ruler hath commissioned us
To blot from off the globe, as once he did
The Jews vile Canaan's brood t' exterminate:
For those contented are with slaughtered foes,
While thou dost strive (but thou shalt miss thy mark)
To wring two hearts with everlasting pangs,
And in a furnace of unending woe

To plunge a household, happy but for thee!
Thou miscreant too black for Satan's realm,
I challenge thee to prove thy wretched words!"
"Enough! Thine epithets fall harmlessly
As wasted breath upon the stately oak.
I have spoke truth; how else should I pronounce
These names, unknown to all but me and thee, —
These names of Eva and of Juliet,
Which thou thyself hadst well-nigh lost from thought?
When, parting in two bands, as thou didst see,
My copper-colored brethren took their course
In two directions, — thou with one didst go,
But Eva, with the other and with me,
Came to the village of my native tribe.
There have I seen her growth; there wooed I her;
Thence fled she, when thou wrenchedst her from me.
So thou, not I, her husband hast become;
I wish thee joy of thy right noble prize!
More satisfaction hath this hour to give,
At witness of thy happy honeymoon,
Than if myself were bridegroom! Fare thou well!"
Then quickly strode the Indian out of view,
While, wrapt in anguish and despair, stood Ralph,
With horror all his senses stupefied.

But sudden impulse roused him from his trance.
"With death before thine eyes thou wilt recant,"
He muttered to himself; and straight he sought
The means of apprehending him who thus

Had shattered in one moment life's best dreams.
In drunken revel and in deep debauch
They found and seized him; when the fumes were spent,
He woke to find himself with murder charged.
Ralph visited him within his gloomy cell.
"If thou art Half-Breed Jack," he said, "I saw
Thee drown my infant sister in the brook.
Thy neck is forfeit to the hangman's noose
If thou dost not thy frightful tale revoke.
Say but that word, and thou art free. Beware
How thou dost trifle with a man deep-wronged!"
The culprit started; then he turned his face,
Grown twofold darker with malignity,
To Ralph, and hoarsely said: "Why should I seek
To save a life so worthless and forlorn?
All — all I have, and am, and hope to be,
Weighed in the balance with this choice revenge,
Is less than nothing; I can die content;
Thy sister Eva is thy new-made wife!"
"Great God of Heaven, pity!" so prayed Ralph,
As, cold and deathlike, prone upon the floor
He fell.   And thence the jailor bore his form,
And placed him on a bed, and summoned aid
(Mistaken kindliness!) to call back life.
So Ralph revived: but not the same awoke
As when, an hour before, he sank: a change
Utter and awful had passed o'er his brow.
His eyes were lustreless; his face was grave,
And sad, and furrowed as with many years;

While, in the brief lapse.of a day and night,
His dark hair was besprinkled as with snow.
All wondered at the shock and asked the cause;
He, mournful, shook his head, but answered not.

Meantime, how fared the winsome bride? She sailed,
In blissful ignorance of these events,
Across the great, mysterious ocean; saw
Day after day succeed, night after night,
While onward ploughed the giant messenger
Between two continents;—dreamed happy dreams,
Thought happy thoughts, planned happy plans;—
Oft said: "The darkest hour precedes the dawn;
The gorgeous sunset is the gift of clouds;
The radiant rainbow follows e'er the storm."
So drove away intrusive fears, and smiled
As though the Future were already hers.
Ah! Gracious Father of our mortal frames,
What were our lives, without immortal hope?

The sea was fair; the winds breathed low and soft;
The firmament revealed God's handiwork
Resplendent; all seemed well. Full soon again
That company should bless the sight of land,
And press with eager feet the Old World's shores.
What if an older world than that they seek, —
What if a brighter shore than that they left, —
Shall erelong greet their vision, where no sea
Doth roll its treacherous waves, or parting come

7

To those deemed worthy of admittance there?
They recked not that it so had been decreed;
They laughed, and sang, and slept dull hours away,
Till transformation of the sky and main
Foretold the coming tempest, — till it broke
In wildest fury on the gallant ship.
Of no avail was skill; in vain were tears
And supplications for divine relief.
The vessel floundered helpless in the trough,
Was tossed upon the high, resistless waves,
Anon plunged into seething depths between;
The cordage shrieked their knell; the howling blast
Their gloomy funeral discourse shouted loud;
The coast they longed for once, now proved their doom
(How many times, O Lord! we pray to thee
For that which Thou canst see would ruin us!);
And, as they struck upon its rocky bounds
With shock terrific, leaped the hissing brine
Above them, tore them from their dying grasp,
And many hurled into eternity.
Of these was Agatha.   Stark on the beach
The hardy landsfolk found her, where the tide
Had cast her; awed and silent, there they stood,
And gazed upon her spiritual face,
And whispered one another: "Ah! how sad
That her young life should be extinguished now
Amid the glad days of her blooming youth!"
But when the simple country pastor said:
"HE knoweth best!" they could but sigh: "Amen!"

The news of the disaster flew with speed
More swift than wings could give; men's hearts were
    bowed
In direst woe, and women's sobs arose
For shipwrecked dear ones, buried in the deep.
One soul alone rejoiced: Ralph read at first,
Half-doubting of its truth, yet kissed the words
That others looked upon with streaming eyes.
"If this might not prove false, O God!" he said;
"If only she is safe in heaven's fold
And never learns—" he shuddered lest some chance
Had saved her; but at last he knew the worst, —
The best, —and praised his Maker's name.

Then came the trial of the murderer,
When all men heard his secret. There he rose
Within the dock, and pleaded guilt, and told
In accents harsh the bitter truth in full.
And Ralph went forth into the open air,
His reason (gift divinest unto man,
Yet in such case a blessing better lost)
Dethroned forever; so the curious crowd,
Smit with commiseration, let him pass
Between their open ranks; and some, though few,
In fleeting tenderness his sorrow shared,
But soon forgot: this world has only room
For each one's private joys and griefs; all else
Is unto each as though it had not been.

At length sweet-scented May renewed once more
The earth, long held in winter's icy bond.
And, as those bleak months, sweeping out of sight
The beauty of their predecessors' reign,
Ralph's altered fortune typified, — his loss
Of all delightsome, — so the vernal warmth
Of the all-potent spring-time, conq'ring death
And raising prostrate life to life again,
Was emblematic of his latest state.
He sank to rest.   What voice shall dare to say,
That He who year by year beneath the snow
Protects the violet, till its hour doth come
To bloom and shed its fragrance all abroad,
Hath not, in Clime where evil never comes,
New-oped the blossom mundane frosts destroyed? —
There where the carnal dross of this low world
Is shaken from their wings, and in the grave,
Together with their mortal frames, is left
To perish with the earthy, — who can know
What joys celestial kindred spirits feel?
Then trust we, that they compensation found;
Then hope we that the Power which rules the skies,
Untrammeled by the gyves of time and sense,
United in angelic love these hearts
That here were crushed, and made them blest for aye!

POEMS.

SEMI-CENTENNIAL OF LOWELL.[1]

I.

"ARMS do I sing!" the Latin poet[2] cries,
And in majestic measure to our eyes
Unfolds the glittering panoply of wars,
The deeds of blood-stained heroes, and their scars.
Full oft have other poets, small and great,
Called down the Muses from their lofty state,
Lines to indite with crimson-colored pen,
To chant sweet strains and drown the wail of men.
Not thus to-day would we implore their aid ;
Better, by far, the task alone essayed
In mortal weakness, without heavenly fire,
Our hearts to quicken and our tongues inspire.
Yet one there is among the Sisters Nine,
Whose melody is none the less divine, —

[1] Celebrated March 1, 1876.
[2] Virgil.

Thalia called, — in whom dwells kindly love :
A gentle daughter, sprung from Thundering Jove.
Her would we seek to be a guest this day,
And with her potent influence grace our lay.
Not then shall martial sounds engross our mind ;
But, with our grateful thoughts towards Heaven inclined,
The angel host our very souls shall thrill
With the glad message, " Peace on earth ! good will ! "

II.

An Eastern legend, writ for childish ear,
Relates (what you will scarce believe, I fear)
That there was once a mat, of virtue rare,
Which swiftly bore its owner through the air
For countless leagues, o'er river, mountain, sea,
Concealed from others, and from danger free.
A richer prize than this we all may claim,
And Memory, void of magic, is its name.
With speed of thought it bridges over time,
And wafts us gently to another clime.
I pray you, now, embark upon its wings,
And backward fly, till into sight it brings
The mysteries of Fifty Years Agone,
When into life this goodly town was born.
Review, with me, the hallowed scenes of yore,
Assured that none the journey will deplore.

III.

When the ancient Roman mother held her child upon her knee,
Him she taught to worship Jove and "Father Tiber" reverently.

Prostrate falls the pagan Hindoo on the mighty Ganges' banks;
From it earthly blessings craveth, to it rendereth his thanks.
Egypt's swarthy sons and daughters homage paid to sluggish
 Nile,
As the Christian seeks devoutly for his Heavenly Father's smile.
And, although these sacred honors our unsentient streams must
 lack,
Yet the welkin loud shall echo of the lordly Merrimack;
Ring, the skies, with shout exultant for the placid Concord's
 tide;
For Lowell is the natural offspring of this happy groom and
 bride!
Thus while we, with hearts o'erflowing, celebrate our Jubilee,
They, together softly gliding, whisper of us to the sea;
Proudly boast us as their best-loved, yet forget not as they sport
Their three other buxom daughters—Lawrence, Haverhill,
 Newburyport.
Children these of whom they well may quote Cornelia's fond
 reply:
"These our jewels are, O Nations! Lucre these could never
 buy!"
Filial gratitude return we! May their life-blood never cease,
And the passing years bring naught to interrupt their wedded
 peace!

IV.

"Glorious things of thee are spoken, Zion, City of our God!"
Sang the psalmist in his rapture, as famed Salem's streets he
 trod.

8

And, as we shall scan the features of the sturdy little band
Who with patience laid foundations here forevermore to stand,
Start those words with honest impulse, unrestrained by doubts
    or fears,
As with fadeless bays we crown them, withered not by lapse of
    years.
They upreared no splendid Temple, such as David's vision
    viewed;
Offered up no sacrifices; reveled not in plenitude;
They built not around our borders mural walls of massive stone,
Nor the Presence of Jehovah claimed to be with them alone;
But with humble, modest labor sought to benefit their race,
Quite content if fickle Fortune did not wholly hide her face.
"Beautiful for situation, joy of earth shall this be called!"
Was the language of their firm faith, by no obstacle appalled.
Ay! if he has earned our tributes who has caused from earth
    to spring
Only one slight blade of grass, in spot where erst was no green
    thing,
Think you not those men and women have eternal praises won,
That shall swell in future ages and the conqueror's fame outrun?
Priest and Prophet, Sage and Warrior, each may win a wide
    renown,
But he earns a nobler pæan who in peace doth plant a town!

v.

No demi-god, or nursling of the wolf,
    Laid deep and strong the bases of our homes;

We burn no incense to their memories;
   No mausoleum towers above their tombs;
No sculptured column tells their gallant deeds
   In glowing verse to heedless passers-by;
But on our walls their graces are inscribed,
   And from our hearts their names shall never die.

Who can forget the men who cast their all —
   Their art, their industry, their moderate wealth —
Within the balance of stern Destiny,
   And won her bounties not by secret stealth;
But with the brawny arm, the active mind,
   The consecrated soul and tireless will,
Strove here to bless their fellow humankind,
   Together raising Church, and School, and Mill!

Then laurels render unto Hale and Boott,
   To Lawrence, Jackson, Appleton and Hurd!
Giants were they among the sons of men,
   And, like th' Apostles, grand in deed and word.
Let praise be sung to Howe and Whipple quaint;
   To Dutton, Moody, and their comrades all,
To Nesmith, Francis, Worthen, Colburn: these
   Shall future generations high extol.
Yet chief among them our godfather stands,
   Like Saul amid the Hebrew congregation;
And Francis Cabot Lowell's name shall live —
   A household word and lasting inspiration!

VI.

Fast rose the structures of colossal size,
   By men of genius guided, such as these,
Till spindle, loom, and shuttle ready stood
   To execute the mind's sublime decrees.
They dedicated not to frowning gods
   Their skill: no vestal virgins fed the fire
To satiate a mystic deity
   And turn away his dreaded, vengeful ire.

No! these were temples, but not futile ones,
   To superstition nurse, and blind the soul:
Temples were they for man's advantage plann'd,
   And served by priestesses not clad in stole!
God dwelleth not in houses made with hands,
   When decked with human pride and vain display,
But wheresoe'er He finds a suppliant heart,
   And where *man's good* is sought from day to day.

VII.

To those who love the Lord, saith Holy Writ,
   And, loving Him, their brother-man do love,
All things shall work together toward good,
   And even seeming evil useful prove.
To-day our city is a monument
   That emphasizeth well that blissful faith;
For though dark clouds have ofttimes lowered round,
   Right on and upward hath she trod her path.

From wilderness, where roamed the dusky band
   Of Wamesits, whom Eliot yearned to save ;
From rural precinct which the generous towns
   Of Chelmsford, Tewksbury, and Dracut gave;
From low estate as village, have we grown
   By swift degrees to city rank and station —
Proud of our history, our mammoth mills,
   Our maidens fair, and — of our population !

When rang the tocsin of the dreadful strife
   That for a time armed brother against brother,
First offering made we for the Nation's life,
   And first foul Treason leaped our sons to smother.
But when sweet Peace once more returned to earth,
   And sheathed the sword too long imbrued in gore,
None learned more quickly to forgive the wrong,
   And heal the gaping wound forevermore !

VIII.

Praise God ! our Fiftieth Anniversary
   Brings no forebodings to us, of decay;
No deadly fever lurks within our veins, —
   No slow consumption wastes our strength away.
Clear is our brain ; our conscience free from guile ;
   Our hands are busy as the tossing main ;
We stand upon the very verge of youth,
   A loftier pinnacle resolved to gain.

The lesson of the Past we read with joy;
  The retrospective view most fair appears;
And, catching up the armor of the dead,
  We look with hope far into coming years.
Thus far the Lord hath bountifully blessed:
  Let this our confidence and faith enhance.
Our puny hand in His, so strong, we place,
  And sound the word along the line — "Advance!"

ILLUSION.

BESIDE the rolling Merrimack —
Famed in the annals of two stranger races,
Though one has passed away and left few traces —
    At eve I trod a beaten track.

A single star peeped from the sky ;
The cricket shrilled his merry-solemn measure,
Imparting to my soul a mournful pleasure,
    As dreamily I passed him by.

Across the darkly flowing wave
Loomed indistinctly, in the twilight gloaming,
What to my fancy, like my footsteps, roaming,
    Seemed castle proud and fortress brave.

Anon their gleam along the walls
A thousand rays with brilliant scintillations ;
The picture all the magic transformations
    Of Oriental tales recalls.

Assuredly so fair a home,
Whose outward semblance rivals Eastern splendor,
Must shelter noble lords and ladies tender,
    To whom fell sorrow ne'er doth come.

Then I remembered me of when
I passed, one day, within those grimy portals,
And saw the toiling, weary, heart-sick mortals,
    Wee children, pallid maids, and men.

" Ah me ! "   I thought, and sadly sighed ;
" 'T was thus in youth I strolled beside Time's current,
And saw bright castles, with a vision fervent,
    Which proved but mills, by daylight tried."

BALTIMORE.[1]

— — — —

BLACK-VISAGED Treason now hath raised his hand
And sent his challenge through the startled land.
The Ensign of the Free on Sumter's walls
Before his belching cannon, shuddering, falls,
While Anderson's staunch handful loth retire,
Their fortress, as their bursting hearts, on fire.
The loyal Nation, waking from its dream
Of false security, leaps to redeem
Its stronghold and its honor at a blow,
And strike the fratricide aggressor low.

[1] The Sixth Massachusetts Regiment of Volunteers, in passing through Baltimore, Md., on their way to defend Washington, D. C., April 19, 1861, lost the first blood in the late rebellion, and four of their number were killed by a mob. This poem relates that event; while the succeeding one commem-orates a reunion in Baltimore, April 19, 1880, of the survivors of that conflict, who were handsomely entertained by the Baltimoreans, with many sentiments of regret for the past and reconciliation for the future.

Most quick to rally from the earthquake shock, —
Firm-rooted in her faith as Plymouth Rock, —
The Old Bay State responded to the call
Which Lincoln issued to the Northland all,
And sent her truest sons, her richest blood,
To still the rising storm and quell the flood.
Her Wilson and her Sumner spoke the word ;
Her Andrew summoned her to draw the sword ;
Her Schouler and her Butler rose in might,
And forth she hastened to the ghastly fight.
From plough and pulpit, desk and school and loom,
Sprang patriot youths, to meet untimely doom ;
The bridegroom tore himself from tender charms,
Unmindful of aught else but deadly arms ;
Deep sobs of parting mingled with the clang
Of flashing weapons, each a tiger's fang
Athirst for prey, regardless of who weeps,
Or who the never-ending slumber sleeps,
So only that fair Freedom be preserved,
For which each heart is steeled, each hand is nerved.

Forth from the peaceful scenes of Middlesex,
From field and valley which the spring-bud decks,
And forth from cities of the Merrimack,
Have marched proud heroes, never to come back.
Theirs were the sires, a century before,
Who crimsoned Lexington with British gore ;
Theirs was the heritage those fathers gave,
And theirs the vow its threatened hope to save !

The clouds of April showered gracious tears,
In sympathy with human doubts and fears,
As o'er the pavement blue-clad columns passed,
Whereon those footfalls were of some the last.
Then out of Boston swept that valiant band —
The gallant Sixth, with stern Jones in command ;
Sped swiftly toward the Capital afar,
To bear the siege and brunt of horrid war.
Each cheek was flushed with ardent aims, and high ;
Each pulse beat gladly; nobly beamed each eye ;
No lip was blanched, no breath was faint with dread,
Nor faltered those who soon must join the dead ;
With holy purpose every breast was thrilled,
And each submissive to whate'er God willed.
Come weal or woe, come triumph or defeat,
They all with Cicero could cry, " 'T is sweet
And blessed for one's Fatherland to die ! "
And dared do all things save from danger fly.

Full soon with serried ranks they eager stand
Beside the portal of fair Maryland,
And seek a passage over her domain,
Beleaguered Washington that they may gain.
But, as they knock without their sister's gate,
Responses harsh their doubting ears await:
" Not thus our soil shall Northern troops invade,
Though Liberty and Union be betrayed ;
Our paths are sacred ; homeward turn again ;
State Rights we value o'er the Rights of Men ! "

In vain the protest there should come no ill ;
The stubborn answer was refusal still.
Short time for parley could they then afford ;
Across her borders the defenders poured,
Decorous all, intent to work no harm,
Fierce opposition striving to disarm.
So Baltimore they reached, where fate ordained
The streets with righteous life-blood should be stained.

The lurid tempest gathered in their track ;
A howling mob essayed to drive them back.
They heard the premonitions of the storm ;
They saw the thunder-surcharged cloudbanks form ;
Yet on they pressed, prepared to meet the worst,
Till on their heads devote the whirlwind burst.
Around them quickly flew the furious stones,
That smote with grievous force their aching bones ;
From windows o'er them coward foes concealed
Discharged a fatal volley, till they reeled
And swayed, but still advanced with measured pace,
Determination seated on each face.
They dealt their enemies rude blow for blow,
Repaying shot with shot, their souls aglow ;
So thus at length resistance overcame,
And won the laurel of eternal fame.
Yet victory was bought at heavy cost :
Four chivalrous New England lives were lost.
They fell in bloom of Youth, in Manhood's prime,

Destroyed by hateful murder ere their time.
So saintly Abel, smit in anger, died,
And, like to his, their blood for vengeance cried ;
So Stephen sank before the rabble's wrath,
And so their spirits trod the upward path.
Not e'en the fiery pomp Elijah knew,
When to the sky celestial chargers drew
His chariot, in Elisha's ravished sight,
Beamed more refulgent with a sacred light !

There in the city of his death lies one —
Brave Taylor, of a kindred unbeknown ;
In Lawrence, Needham's ashes find repose,
Where gently o'er his grave the zephyr blows ;
And here, where Lowell's toilsome pulses beat,
Sleep Ladd and Whitney in their last retreat.
Maine and New Hampshire gave their vital breath,
And Massachusetts treasures them in death.
But though far parted were their childhood homes,
And though thus distant are their scattered tombs,
One cause they loved, one tragic end they found,
One common Country shall their dirge resound.
A Nation mourned their loss, and still laments,
And yearly gathers round their monuments,
With tender hands full-laden, to array
Their resting-places with the flow'rs of May.
These voice our faith, our gratitude and love ;
They breathe of Immortality above.

E'en as the Angel at Christ's sepulchre
Saluted Mary, when she brought sweet myrrh
And spices aromatic, — so these say
To us who linger near the tomb to-day :
" Seek not the living here ; for, though they died,
They have arisen and are glorified ! "

MASSACHUSETTS AND MARYLAND.

I.

"My word is law! I reign by right divine,
Where'er the sun doth on a Briton shine,
Or where a subject race doth bow the knee
In New France, India, or isles of the sea!"
So spake King George the Third, in boastful pride,
And "Amen!" loud his Parliament replied.
In vain a Chatham's eloquence implored
To rule by Constitution, not by Sword ;
In vain great Burke and Fox their voices raised :
The monarch's passion only higher blazed.
"Fly ye across the ocean, swiftly fly,
To where my wide possessions fruitful lie ;
Straight from my Colonies a tribute bring,
For they are bound in duty to their king :
Their charter rights, their gold, the land they till,
Are mine, and they but hold them at my will !"
So cried the tyrant ; and forthwith a horde
Of myrmidons upstarted at the word.

"Thine, all!" responded Parliament; and "Thine, all!"
Echoed in peasant's hut and lordly hall.
Then o'er the deep the tax-collectors sped,
To *stamp* out freedom with their iron tread.

II.

But, hark!   What sound is that which greets their ears,
As three-hilled Boston on their sight appears?
"No right divine, but that of God above!
No tax that we ourselves do not approve!
These western wilds our rugged strength hath wrought,
And out of chaos into beauty brought;
Our valor hath the savage Red Man curbed,
And we can gaze on Red-Coats undisturbed!
Our king we honor; but our English name
By cringing cowardice we will not shame.
Take back your stamps and excise-laws unjust;
Nor seek on freemen such disgrace to thrust."
Then quailed the minions, and returned dismayed;
But hotter anger now King George displayed.
"My word is law!   I reign by right divine!
Crush out these rebels that have dared repine.
They prate of fealty, but brave my power;
Before my armies they shall quickly cower.
Forth, to my ships!   Cross once again the sea,
And bid them die, if they would still be free!"
Heaven heard the threat in silence; earth grew still,
As Man rose up, his brother's blood to spill.

So sky and earth are wont to show false calm,
Ere bursts the fury of the tropic storm.

III.

Thou, Massachusetts, first shalt bear the blow,
And all the terrors of dread warfare know;
Thy sons and daughters from their homes shall flee,
And wrapped in flames those cherished homes shall see;
The foeman's steel shall to thy vitals pierce,
And o'er thee ravage British cohorts fierce.
But not alone the agony is thine,
Nor singly doth thy star of glory shine:
To North, to South, companions of thy woes,
Twelve kindred Colonies shall feel thy throes.
Not least of these in loyalty and love,
Fair Maryland an able aid shall prove.
Though feminine of name, yet only so;
Another Boadicea she doth show,
Or like the female wolf that sucklings nursed,
Who founded Rome, among republics first.
Her sons around the standard of the brave
Joined Massachusetts' heroes, and one grave
In many a struggle for a nation's life
They filled together, past all earthly strife.
One boasts of Concord and of Bunker Hill,
And tells of Lexington a tale to thrill.
The other hath an equal claim for praise,
And wears as bright, though not so blood-stained, bays;
Her soldiers fought on other battle-ground

10

Than that herself did furnish, and the sound
Of cannon-roar and musket smote the air
In other parts; but none the less her share
Of pain and sorrow while these long endured —
Of triumph, when the guerdon was secured;
Her hearths were desolate, her widows mourned,
Her orphans wailed for fathers unreturned.
If Massachusetts have her Faneuil Hall,
So Maryland points to her capital,
And tells how to Annapolis repaired
Those sires who early the resolve declared
That free and independent States should rise
From out the ashes of the Colonies.
And when the Congress ratified the deed,
And abrogation of the king decreed;
Gave to the world the story of their wrong;
Appealed to God to side not with the strong;
And for the issue pledged each other there
Lives, fortune, sacred honor: lo! how fair
To us, their offspring, on the precious scroll
Those names which Massachusetts did enroll!
And, following close, the sons of Maryland
To Freedom's Magna Charta set their hand.
When laud we Hancock, Adams (Sam and John),
Laud we, too, Carroll, him of Carrollton;
When meed we pay to Gerry and to Paine,
To Chase, to Stone, and Paca raise a strain.
No single arm, no single State, could hope
With Britain's mighty energies to cope;

But Maryland and Massachusetts gave
Each to the other strength to help and save ;
Clasped hand in hand, merged heart and soul in one,
Till the invader fled, — the task was done.

IV.

Nor ceased she then, that southern helpmeet true :
For when, in later years, a British crew
Again in arms appeared upon our strand,
They met a sharp rebuff from Maryland ;
Ross tried the *metal* of her Baltimore,[1]
The which he had deep reason to deplore.
And, as an earnest that 'twas not for greed
That she had striven in mighty word and deed,
She gave a portion of her rare domain,[2]
That there the Nation might a homestead gain.

V.

Not short of heaven is bliss without alloy ;
Night follows light, and weeping quenches joy.
So fell it, on one sad and solemn day,
That Discord came to drive sweet Peace away.
State against state arose, in mortal hate,
And trembling in the balance hung our fate.
To thee, O Maryland ! our eyes did turn,
To see if thine alliance thou wouldst spurn,

[1] September, 1814.
[2] District of Columbia.

Forget thy first love, a new choice to make,
And on secession all thy future stake.
Not long thou kept'st the loyal in suspense ;
Not long thou gavest reason of offense.
As Massachusetts was not always sound
In all her members, but e'en there were found
Room for a Shays' rebellion,[1] room for mobs, —
Children who caused her breast to heave with sobs —
So thou wert cumbered : so thy head was bent
In anguish for what thou couldst not prevent.
We chide thee not ; we mind us how the Lord
Bade him to cast the stone at her abhorred,
The woman sinful, who no sin had known ;
We think that never at the Great White Throne
Could mortal stand, arrayed in robes of heaven,
If means had not been found to be forgiven.
Thank God ! thou didst not leave us, though thine arm
One moment faltered and inflicted harm.
Quick to repent thou wast, and shed the tear
Of pity o'er our youthful martyrs' bier.
There, where he fell, sleeps one of those we sent ;
And thou hast reared o'er him a monument,
And paid his dust that tender reverence
Which to the dead is our sole recompense.
If aged Priam, 'reft of his support,
Could unto stern Achilles' tent resort,
And, for that Hector had a funeral pile,

[1] 1786-7.

Could on the slayer of his children smile ;
The while the festive bowl passed round the board,
And Greek and Trojan sheathed the reeking sword :
Assuredly, in Gospel age and land,
We can extend the cordial, open hand,
Condone the past, blot out the erring score,
And swear eternal faith, to end no more !
There, by that grave which hath its counterpart
In Lawrence and in Lowell's busy mart ;
There, where sleeps Taylor in the silent dust,
The living we would greet with words of trust.

VI.

Long years agone (so History relates),
Where flourish now rich kingdoms and estates,
The Druid patriarchs their mystic rites
Performed, adoring sun and stellar lights.
And oft, when rage possessed some heathen clan
To visit carnage on their neighbor-man,
E'en as the tribes stood ready for the fray,
Threatening and awful in grim war's array ;
The priests and priestesses, unarmed and frail,
Strode in betreen : the combatants turned pale,
In presence of Religion dared not smite,
But bowed in worship where they thought to fight !
Shall, then, the pagan Briton and the Gaul
In piety and mercy us forestall ?
No ! no ! A thousand times we answer, No !

Our Christian brother shall not be our foe !
Love shall unite us closer than before,
And hearts estranged shall melt in Baltimore !

VII.

Land of the Pilgrims ! swept by wintry blasts !
Long as thy Plymouth Rock the storm outlasts,
So long shall Maryland thine ally be,
So firm her faith and plighted constancy.
Land of the Sunny South ! long as thy streams
Shall gently flow where balmy zephyr dreams,
So long shall hardy Massachusetts stand
Defender of the fame of Maryland.
Each shall in each much complemental find,
As Eden's pair all excellence combined :
No holier tie bound Adam to his bride :
Whom God hath joined, let no man dare divide !

THE SNOW.

THE earth was naked and brown, one night ;
When morning dawned it was clad in white ;
And as Phœbus beheld it from heaven once more,
A garment bespangled with jewels it wore.

An old man gazed on the transformed scene —
On the gleaming forest and river's sheen —
And he thought, as he mused upon years long flown,
" Nature a shroud o'er the earth hath thrown.

" The leaves are vanished, the flowers dead,
The beautiful verdure of summer is fled ;
This mantle of snow, which my sight doth greet,
Enfoldeth the world as a winding-sheet."

A young wife smiled at the change, and said :
" The earth in its bridal attire is arrayed ;
Dull labor and toil for a time flee away,
For Nature is keeping a holiday."

Beside a cot knelt a mother fair,
Who watched o'er the little one slumbering there ;
And concerning the snow to herself she said :
" Dame Nature her children has tucked in bed.

"Asleep are the flowers ; and around each form
This cov'ring is wrapped, to protect from all harm.
When the morning of spring o'er the earth shall break,
The kiss of the sunbeams each blossom will wake."

THE FISHERS.

On Galilean waters long had toiled
   Two humble brethren with the fisher's net.
Their brows were reddened by the sun's fierce glare,
   And with the midnight dew their locks were wet.
Scant were their wages, for the finny prey
   Was often shy of all their cunning craft,
And oft they hungered, as through weary hours
   Their seines alone rewarded every draught.

What poet, with a vision keen and clear,
   Directed by the Muses from on high —
What limner, with a fancy all aglow —
   What prophet, learning wisdom from the sky —
Could in these lowly lives aught noble find,
   Or heroes make of stock so mean and poor?
What sorcerer transmute the paltry twain
   To more than kings, by Egypt's mystic lore?

There walked upon the beach, one happy morn,
   A Man Divine, who looked upon the pair.
His heart was aching for a sin-sick world,

11

Whose awful burden He alone could bear.
He knew all souls; He read all destinies;
   Beneath their rude exterior He saw
Two precious gems; and He whose potent will
   From chaos called the earth and every star; —

At whose Almighty mandate healing light
   Dispelled thick primal darkness and deep gloom,
Spoke words of comfort to their spirits faint,
   And to a grander work He bade them come.
"No longer cast your nets upon the sea,
   For prize so trifling," cried the Master then;
"Leave now your boats and follow after Me,
   For I will make you fishers of lost men!"

With prompt obedience to the holy call,
   They straightway Christ's disciples chose to be.
Forsaking all attachments of the past,
   They dared all dangers in His company;
Learned sweetest precepts from His lips inspired;
   To death attended Him, and felt it meet
That they should not above their Lord be blessed,
   Whose wounded side they preached, and nail-pierced feet.

Their lot seemed bitter to their taunting foes;
   Their zeal seemed futile, and their hope forlorn;
Their King with malefactors early died;
   Their symbol was His Cross and Crown of Thorn.
To human eye, they labored vainly still
   As when all night they drew their empty nets;

But God was with them, and their cause was His:
  To-day the sun upon their fame ne'er sets.

The deeds of potentates who flourished then
  Have perished from remembrance; scarce are known
The names of persecutors whom they braved —
  Tyrants who sat upon a Godless throne.
But these poor peasantry, who left their all
  And gave their lives, to help a ruined race,
By history immortal, round the globe,
  In foremost rank of heroes have their place.

Sin in all ages works with equal woe;
  Christ in all ages calls for fishermen;
In every age they answer His appeal,
  And round Him gather o'er and o'er again.
On life's tempestuous billows forth they ride,
  By twos and threes, or joyous groups they form,
And seek to rescue from the yawning gulf
  The hapless victims of Temptation's storm.

God speed thee in thy mission, loving heart,
  If singly thou dost breast the raging sea !
God bless thy labors, noble band of youth,
  If hand with hand ye join in ministry !
If souls ye pluck from out the fatal stream
  That o'er the precipice leaps wildly down,
Stars of rejoicing in a higher sphere
  Shall each one prove upon your victor's crown.

LAKE MOOSELUCMAGUN,TIC.[1]

WHEN low the autumn sun adown the sky
  Reluctantly hath passed, and fain would stay
  To gaze and smile upon thy face alway,
Thy bosom quivers with a gentle sigh ;
Thou seest that within his ardent eye
  Which tinges thy fair cheek with rosy hue.
  So would I, in my modest maiden true,
Revealed in tell-tale blush, her thought descry.
  Then would I haste, if fate compelled awhile
    From her pure presence, as yon sun his course,
    To look again within her eyes' deep blue ;
Not all the world beside should me beguile,
    But e'er impelled by Love's resistless force,
      Each morn my homage should be paid anew !

---

[1] One of the Rangeley group, in Maine.

TO MOUNT WASHINGTON.

—— ——

I GAZE in admiration on thy Titan form,
   O Mount, that bearest Washington's great name!
   And every title else for thee seems tame —
Alike majestic in the calm, or raging storm.
But, as all hearts forever tow'rd that Leader warm
   Who gave thy patronymic, that he chose
   No monarch's rank, but o'er ambition rose,
And hath the Father of a People Free become ; —
   So thee I would not label King ; a higher
   Renown and appellation thine shall be :
      I hail thee Father of free-bounding streams !
For many laughing daughters claim thee sire,
   Which merrily glide onward to the sea,
      Fair as the images that rise in dreams.

BUT FOR A SEASON.

———

MYSTERIOUS are the ways of Providence
And past our finding out ; yet this we know,
Reflecting on the path where He has caused,
In all our weary past, our steps to go :
  All things He doeth well.

Faint is our vision ; yet beyond the Grave
Rise glorious shapes, whose former mortal face,
E'en moulded in dull clay, we madly loved,
Endowed more beauteous now with heavenly grace.
Mists of this life shut out the blessed view,
Alas ! But Faith assists us to peer through.
  No longer let grief swell.

Comes now the day with haste when we shall walk
On fields of bliss, and ope our happy eyes,
Look forth from just-awakened slumbers sweet,
Behold our lost ones with a glad surprise —
  Yes ! ne'er to say " Farewell ! "

DROWNED.

THY light went out amid no circling friends ;
　Thy pallid brow no mother bathed with tears ;
Thy dying look no glimpse of heaven lends
　To eyes that fain would pierce their veil of fears.
In hour whose shadow threw no portent dark
　Across the sunny path which thou didst tread,
The sombre boatman near thee moored his bark,
　And bore thy soul untimely to the dead.

The sun in skies serene no paler grew,
　But mortal cheeks turned ashen when 't was told ;
No shudder stirred the leaves, the forest through,
　But hearts were swept with anguish uncontrolled.
The fair world bloomed with freshness, as before ;
　No pall was cast athwart the verdant fields ;
But grief to gladness now has closed the door,
　And earth awhile no joy or pleasure yields.

Yet, hark !   There floats upon the stilly air,
   In accents graced by angel minstrelsy,
A thought of sadder mourning and despair
   For others, lost in gloomier depths than he.
Ah ! weeping ones !   The bitter waves of sin
   Are hopeless as the very lake of hell.
Be thankful that the gurgling waters' din
   O'er body only played its funeral knell !

On earth the treacherous billows parted wide
   To swallow all the heart most richly prized :
Beyond our vision, from the crystal tide
   Emerged a radiant spirit, new-baptized !
No dew of death, no dampness of the stream,
   Clung to his locks, nor drenched his garments white.
Safe on that shore he stands, fair as a dream,
   Where dying endeth and there is no night.

MEMORIAL DAY.

"Greater love hath no man than this, that a man lay down his life for his friend." — *Jesus.*

"Dulce et decorum pro patria mori." — *Cicero.*

WE turn to-day from accustomed cares,
    To sing of the loved and lost,
To mingle our praise, and tears, and prayers,
    O'er a mighty holocaust.
From the busy marts of tireless trade,
    From the bustling streets of the town,
Our willing feet have with sadness strayed
    Where the dead have laid them down.

Not when the blighting autumnal frosts
    Dark gloom to our bosoms bring,
Do we gather where sleep the gallant hosts ;
    But now, in the gladsome spring.
Like leaves from the branches torn away,
    They were swept from each fireside ;

12

But in faith they donned grim war's array,
　And in triumphs of faith they died.

Then May be the month we dedicate
　To recount all their sacrifice,
And with May's bright blossoms we'll decorate
　The spot where each hero lies.
Thrice sweet be their dreamless slumber here,
　And soft be their couches low!
We would cherish them still, and their names revere,
　Though they left us long ago.

O blue be the sky where their spirits dwell!
　Green be the sward o'er each breast!
For Justice and Mercy they valiantly fell, —
　They have entered the soldier's rest.
May they see from abodes of Eternal Peace,
　Where conflict can ne'er intrude,
That their deeds fade not, but e'er increase
　In their country's gratitude.

The flowers we bring to their resting-place
　Must wither beneath the sun,
And the breezes of summer and fall efface
　What to-day we have tenderly done.
But not in the rose or the evergreen,
　O, not in the wild-flower's bloom,
Our measure of love is completely seen,
　To end with their brief perfume.

Perennial grow in our inmost heart,
  Unswept by chill winter's breath,
Affection's forget-me-nots, which no art
  Of a cold world weakeneth.
They were sown when dear ones went from hence,
  They were watered with bitter tears,
And through cloud and in sunshine, constant since,
  They have thrived with the passing years.

Not they alone who marched side by side
  With the fallen, 'mid cannons' roar,
But now are spared, with a comrade's pride
  To bedeck these mounds once more,
May claim this beautiful rite to pay
  To the memory of the dead ;
For a Nation redeemed, no less than they,
  Has a sacred tear to shed.

Alas ! were it not that the Boys in Blue,
  With intrepid souls, and brave,
Marched forth to death where destruction flew,
  And for Freedom their life-blood gave ;
Not now could we boast of Liberty
  And the Equal Rights of Man :
Our land would yet bear the infamy
  Of Slavery's monstrous ban.

Not the Home of the Free could we proclaim
  Our proud Columbia's shore

To all the oppressed of every name,
    Had they faltered in that hour.
But they dared not a shattered land bequeath,
    Inherited one from the sires,
And vowed that their swords they would not sheath
    Till success or the grave were theirs.

It was fated that some should surrender life
    On the sunny Southern slopes ;
But although we wept at the cruel strife,
    We abandoned not our hopes.
And so, at last, through the battle's smoke,
    When our homes had been ravaged sore,
The welcome beams of the glad sun broke,
    And our country was saved evermore.

Thanks be unto God ! Though oft we mourn
    And sigh at the vacant chair,
We would not have our dead return
    At the cost of a fame so fair.
Nor would they come from the realms of shade,
    If the ransom were what they gained ;
For on the altar their lives they laid,
    That the Flag might no more be stained.

There are dead in the South, as well as North,
    And all bow before God's Throne :
So, too, may the living abide henceforth
    In heavenly amity one.

Eternally perish provincial hate !
  Prolong not fraternal broil !
To forgive and forget is divinely great,
  And we have a common soil !

May heaven vouchsafe to our favored land
  A union of hand and heart !
May no estrangement again demand
  That the North and South should part !
The Past is sealed ; and the Future time
  Seems freighted with only joy.
God grant that never shall Treason's crime
  Sweet Harmony seek to destroy !

A CENTENNIAL SENTIMENT.

As the student backward glances through the history of Time,
Every page is red and gory with grim Warfare's deeds of crime.
Nation none is there recorded free from its disastrous blight,
Stifling Love, engendering Passion, prisoning Justice, throning
    Might.

Nobly has our dear Republic sought to fraternize and bind,
With the cords of Christian friendship and forbearance, all man-
    kind.
Battlefields, by her example, ne'er should drink the hero's blood,
But the discords of the nations be adjusted in concord !

Proud we are to be her children ; welcome we each natal-day
Of the principles she fosters — of her glorious liberty.
As the years are swift recurring, loud hosannas we will raise
For her deeds with grace resplendent, worthy of immortal praise.

But when dawns some day united with the memory of Strife,
On which brother-man, remorseless, took a fellow-mortal's life —
Let us silent be and tearful ; let our prayers to God ascend
That the reign of Christ, the Peaceful, soon may come, no more
    to end !

FRATERNITY.

On the bank of a softly-plashing stream
    Lay an army encamped by night;
And many a vision and blissful dream
    To the slumberers brought delight.
The vigilant sentries paced to and fro,
    Or statue-like watched at their post,
While the stars looked down with a mellow glow
    On the weary, unconscious host.

But anon there passed o'er the scene a change;
    For the sentinels cried alarms,
And there came through the darkness a cohort strange,
    As they sprang from their sleep to arms.
Farewell to the pleasure, all too brief,
    Which the moment before they saw!
It must now give place to the awful grief
    And the deeds and the groans of war.

How the angels wept, as they looked from heaven
  On the savage and painful strife !
How swift-throbbing hearts would erelong be riven
  For the loved ones who yielded life !
How the tears of the stalwart survivors rose,
  When the light of the dawning day
Revealed that their comrades, and not their foes,
  They had slain in that cruel fray !

Ah, sad mistake of the midnight hour,
  Oft repeated on sea and land ;
For Man against Man, with relentless power,
  Still raiseth his blood-stained hand.
But there cometh a Morn when hate shall cease,
  In the light of a Father's love,
And the brethren of earth shall unite in peace,
  Like the children of God above !

ODE TO MAJ.-GEN. JOHN STARK.[1]

SILENT, to-day, is the heart of the warrior ;
   Closed is his eagle eye, low 'neath the sod ;
Clasped o'er his gallant breast, bearing no weapon,
   Lie his brave hands, in the peace of his God !
Not in dark aisle of magnificent temple,
   Coffined with monarchs and magnates of earth,
Sleeps he the slumber that knoweth no waking,
   Where human flattery tinsels his worth.

Gently he rests where the breezes do whisper
   Softly above the green couch where he lies ;
Here 'mid the hills which his valor defended,
   Here in the free air, and arched by the skies.
This was the modest spot where he delighted
   Often with Nature to meet and commune ;

---

[1] On the occasion of the re-dedication of his monument, at Manchester,
N. H., May 30, 1876.

13

This was the place where his loved ones he buried :
　Here o'er his grave let bright garlands be strewn.

Honor he craved not, nor high-sounding tributes
　Graved on sarcophagus, chiseled in stone ;
Only the welfare of country he heeded, —
　Sought for the good of his people alone.
Not in his bosom lodged murderous purport ;
　Peace to wild conflict he ever preferred ;
Not in the blood of his kind did he revel,
　Nor by applause was his ambition spurred.

But, when resounded from mountain to mountain
　Summons to arms in dear Liberty's name,
Quickly he sprang from beside the dull ploughshare, —
　Forth to resist the oppressor he came.
Dangers he feared not, nor Death did dismay him ;
　Firm as his native hills towered his soul ;
Conscious that Justice and Right were his safeguards,
　Over his spirit no faltering stole.

Stout were the hearts that acknowledged him chieftain ;
　Sturdy the arms that he led to the fray.
Naught of base malice incited their prowess ;
　Them did the promptings of proud Freedom sway.
Combat is bitter ; yet heaven's glad city
　Rang once with strife and the shock of alarm.

Warfare is sacred, and soldiers are heroes,
 When against evil is raised the strong arm !

Dedicate, then, to the Patriot Leader,
 Column of marble, inscribed with fond lay ;
Consecrate here to a nation of Freemen
 Dust of the Citizen-Soldier, for aye !
Thus will be added no glory or lustre
 Unto a fame that has brightened with years ;
But to ourselves we shall render a duty,
 And show to the World what New Hampshire reveres.

True to her instincts of love for the noble,
 Proud shall she point to her act of this hour,
Disproving the charge of ingratitude's baseness
 Tow'rd those who for her have braved Death's cruel power.
Then long may this monument tell to the reader
 The exploits of Stark, and the pride in his deeds
Which the sons of New Hampshire forever shall nurture,
 So long as her streamlets flow free through her meads.

Better it is that this shaft should be tardy,
 Upreared when its hero had long passed away,
Than that early his merits had thus been emblazoned,
 And then his achievements swift sped to decay.
Better that fame should increase than go backward ;
 Better that love should wait long to express

Its deepest regard, than with haste to display it,
  And soon turn away, some new form to caress !

It is not the Man, but the Spirit, we cherish ;
  It is not the Sword, but a Principle grand,
Which to-day we commemorate, glad and rejoicing, —
  The Patriot's Love in behalf of his land !
We worship no idol ; no homage we offer
  To shades of the dead, though their works we admire.
To God be the glory ! — His arm brought salvation ;
  But to save us He gave us a STARK for our sire !

DEATH THE WAY OF LIFE.

INSTRUCTED so from earliest childhood's year, —
  Conviction pressed upon unwilling mind
  By those whose sway o'er faith was unconfined, —
I long regarded Death with bodeful fear,
And gazed with troubled heart upon the bier.

Unkind and gloomy only seemed the tomb.
  Its rest might be relief from pain and woe,
  But only such as man extinct might know.
I dared not think the time would surely come
When I must own it for a final home.

Each year of life more sad and sombre grew,
  As Time in hasty course the seasons led,
  Passing with eager mien and hurried tread,
And the dread Phantom daily nearer drew —
His spectral face obtruded on my view.

I shuddered oft that, disbelieving God,
  Our primal parents ventured to partake
  Of that which carried in its horrid wake
The visitation of so sore a rod —
The penalty of dreamless sleep beneath the sod.

And am I still oppressed and rendered sad
  By the same cheerless aspect of life's end ?
  Do dire forebodings all my days attend ?
If endless life on earth might now be had
For the mere asking, would my soul be glad?

Ah, no !   I see beyond the Stream of Death
  A Saviour waiting to receive His own ;
  I know that Jordan's tide sweeps near His throne ;
I learn true life begins with man's last breath,
And hope of heaven I have through this blest faith.

Not as a judgment for a wilful deed —
  I now perceive is taught me in the Book —
  Not because mortals God's command forsook,
Was death corporeal set on Adam's seed,
And a relapse to dust 'gainst all decreed.

Nay; but the rather that the sun might beam
  On ceaseless generations of immortal men,

Whose place, when each should fall, might teem again
With others still ; and thus a ceaseless stream
Of souls reach bliss, whom Christ died to redeem.

Death is not a reversion of God's plan ;
   Man does not cease on earth because he sinned ;
   The Evil One had so a victory gained.
The Grave has ever been th' appointed span
'Twixt fleeting and eternal joy, since life began.

TIME.

—

TIME is not an aged pilgrim,
  Snows of centuries round his brow ;
Time is not the Past and Future,
  But the ever-present Now.
Time is not an aged pilgrim,
  Wrinkled, bowed, and gray ;
Time 's an infant, daily dying,
  New-born, day by day !

CHRIST'S TEMPTATION.

ATHWART the eastern hills of fair Judea
　　The early sun began to pour his light,
As two in Salem's Temple mount the stair
　　That leadeth to the dizzy, topmost height.
Strange contrast is apparent in their mien:
　　The one, of gentle step and humble guise;
While he who, walking close beside, is seen,
　　Awakes distrust with darkly rolling eyes.

At length the pinnacle is gained, and far below
　　Stretches the fruitful earth on every hand;
Brightly the waters of the Jordan flow,
　　And by the morning air their brows are fanned.
The streets beneath are silent all, and cold,
　　Save when, at intervals, with hurried tread,
Some care-worn toiler, urged by need of gold,
　　Forestalls the morn to seek his daily bread.

The two gazed downward first, then far away;
　　Proudly that one, but reverently this,

14

As he who lifts his gaze to heaven to pray,
　His mind absorbed in holy state of bliss.
"Art thou the Promised One?" at length exclaimed
　He of the darker look, impatient all;
"Then know'st thou not that of thee it is famed
　Whate'er thou do no evil can befall?

"'T is written in that Psalm which of thee sings,
　That if from here thou cast thyself adown,
The angels safe shall bear thee on their wings,
　Lest thou shouldst dash thy foot against a stone."
"E'en so," arousing from his reverie,
　. Responded his companion, with a sigh;
"Those faithful words were writ concerning me
　By Him who sent me in the world — *to die!*

" But art thou so familiar with the Word,
　And dost not call to mind that warning grave,
'Thou shalt not tempt the Holy God, thy Lord'?
　Why uselessly demand of Him to save?"
With downcast look and half-averted face
　The Tempter sought in vain for a reply,
And turning quickly from the hated place,
　Vanished in mid-air with a vengeful cry.

THE GOLDEN RULE.

Under the walls of Zutphen the English army lay,
As the crouching panther lurketh to leap upon his prey.
Leicester, the lordly chieftain, his heart all steel within,
Counted the tardy hours ere victory he should win.
Little he recked of groanings, little he thought of tears;
Only cared he for glory and the plaudits of distant years.
Never his deeds should perish from Britain's annals brave,
Though his mortal form should moulder to ashes in the grave.

Under the walls of Zutphen the English army lay:
Bitter and yet more bloody the siege grew, day by day.
Thickly the fatal missiles flew hissing through the air,
Many the gallant warriors who sank in death's despair.
Knightlier none waged battle, in all that martial train,
Than courtly Sir Philip Sydney, by unkind fortune slain.
Rueful the tale of his dying; but not of that we sing;
Nobler the act that thrills us than the exploits of a king.

Wounded he lies, and the fever mounts high along his veins;
Thirsting, he gasps for water, as his gore the greensward stains.

Quickly the sparkling nectar is brought, and to his lips
Eager he presses the welcome draught — but not one drop he
    sips;
Pity within his bosom has stirred his inmost soul,
For a soldier, breathing his last, hath set his glazed eyes on the
    bowl.
"Unto this man I yield it," he said, with words divine,
The which all heard with wonder; "*his want is more than mine!*"

Under the walls of Zutphen the English army lay,
Till at length the fortress yielded and ended was the fray.
Unto the mighty Leicester the Netherlanders bowed:
History records his name above the vulgar crowd.
But higher than his is Sydney's, with sacred lustre bright,
Shining from out Oblivion, like the queen-star in the night.
Hero is he who conquered the city for his prize; —
Grander the soul that ruled itself and made deep sacrifice.

TWO MOODS.

As I strolled beside the ocean, high my bosom heaved with awe,
  To behold its dancing billows leap and swell ;
And I gazed with deep emotion on its blue expanse afar,
  While across my soul a sense of grandeur fell.
" I would ever look upon thee," cried I fondly to it then ;
  "I would ever hold communion with thy voice ;
I would catch thy gentle murmur, so unlike the speech of men,
  Or to hear thy mighty roaring would rejoice ! "

But I sailed upon the ocean, when the steamer rocked and rolled ;
  All about me pitched the green and turbid main.
And within I felt commotion ! Ah, such misery untold,
  That I longed devoutly for the land again.
"Oh, a very close acquaintance with thy waves of sickly hue,"
  Then I ruefully exclaimed, " gives me the qualms ;
Thou art beautiful at times, no doubt, but distance, to my view,
  Lends enchantment to thy false, deceptive charms ! "

MUTATION.

I.

"Slow move the lead-shod hours," the maiden sighed ;
  "Long must I tarry ere he come to me."
"O Time, thou halt and lame!" the lover cried,
  "Increase thy pace, that I my sweet may see!"
But Time, with voice decrepit, sad replied,
  "Nay, hearts impatient! nay, it cannot be.
My changeless round a Higher Power doth guide ;
  Nor haste, nor moment's pause, permitteth He."

II.

"Alas, remorseless Time! Thy speed abate,"
  The father importuned, and dropped a tear ;
"One little space turn back thy wheel of fate,
  And spare my child as child another year!"
"O Time," the mother wept, "nor wealth, nor state,
  I ask ; but only leave my infant here —
Here on my bosom!" "Nay, I must not wait,"
  Rejoined the spectre. "On, O Charioteer!"

III.

Beside two graves, where wife and son low sleep,
  The white-locked sire in faith invokes his God :
" I would not, Father, for my lost ones weep,
  Nor wish that life lay all before, untrod.
Time is but servant, and he must needs reap
  And garner up his harvest 'neath the sod ;
But death's fair river he can ne'er o'erleap :
  Eternity shall break his iron rod ! "